Kidnapped

Adapted by Rob Lloyd Jones

Illustrated by Alan Marks

Reading consultant: Alison Kelly
University of Roehampton

In the middle of the 18th century, Scotland was fiercely divided. The clans (tribes) of the Highlands, in the north, were mainly Catholic, and hated the Protestant king, George II. In the south, most 'Lowlanders' supported the King. Many of them regarded Highlanders as wild, savage people. This is the story of a Lowlander, a Highlander, and their incredible adventure…

Usborne Quicklinks

For links to websites where you can find out about Robert Louis Stevenson and his stories, go to the Usborne Quicklinks Website at **www.usborne-quicklinks.com** and enter the keyword 'kidnapped'. Please follow the internet safety guidelines displayed on the Usborne Quicklinks Website. Usborne Publishing is not responsible for the content of any website other than its own.

Contents

Chapter 1

The House of Shaws

There is no finer sight than a Scottish valley on a clear summer morning. Blackbirds swoop through the dawn mist, and the sun lights the heather as if the ground were sprinkled with diamonds.

But I was in mixed spirits that morning, as I walked from Edinburgh to the district of Cramond. My father had died just three weeks earlier. He left me a sealed letter, with an instruction on the front:

To be delivered to Ebenezer Balfour,
of the House of Shaws,
by my son David Balfour.

David Balfour – that's me. And Ebenezer is my uncle. I'd never met him, but had heard that he was a rich lord. I hoped he might give me a new start in life. I dreamed of being a gentleman, with a title after my name.

But, when I reached my uncle's house later that day, my heart sank. It was a miserable building. All of the windows were broken, and crows perched like gargoyles on their crumbling ledges. Was this the place on which I had pinned my hopes?

I continued, determined to deliver my father's letter. No lights flickered inside, and no smoke rose from the crooked chimney.

I knocked on the door. At first, there was no reply. Then, to my horror, a gun poked through one of the windows – aimed at me!

A man's face appeared in the window – round and wrinkled, like a walnut. "Who are you?" he said, in a shrill voice.

"My name is David Balfour," I replied, hoping I sounded braver than I felt. "I have a letter for you from my father."

I noticed the gun shake in the man's grip.

"I'll…I'll let you in," he said. "Wait there."

The door creaked open on rusty hinges. A chill ran down my back when I saw the man properly. He looked like a ghost in rags – with pale skin, sunken eyes, and a long shirt that was tattered and filthy. I knew this must be my uncle, because there were clearly no servants, nor anyone else, in his decrepit house.

"Come inside," he grunted.

He led me down a gloomy corridor, and into a bare kitchen. A fire crackled in the hearth, but the room was icily cold. He offered me a bowl of porridge, which I ate hungrily.

"So, you've come after my money have you?" he croaked.

I rose from the table, angry at his accusation. "I am no beggar, sir! My father is dead, and I came with his letter."

As I spoke, I thought I saw my uncle smile. Was he pleased that his brother had died?

Suddenly, he snatched the letter from my hand. He read it quickly, then tossed it into the fire.

"Don't get upset, Davie," he said. "That letter asked me to look after you, and I shall. But first, you must sleep."

He showed me to a room that was even
colder than the kitchen. The walls glistened
with damp, and cockroaches scurried around
the floor. But before I could protest, he
slammed the door and locked me in.

"Good night, nephew!" he yelled.

I was too tired to complain. I pulled my
coat around me, and curled up on the bed.

Chapter 2

Tricked!

I lay awake for most of the night, shivering from the cold, and listening to the hollow moan of the wind over the hills.

Next morning, when I heard the door being unlocked, I was ready to shout at my uncle. But he gripped my arm with a wrinkly hand.

"I am sorry for last night, Davie," he said. "I mean to help you. You are family, after all."

Again, I saw a cunning smile flash across his face. I did not trust him at all.

Breakfast was another bowl of porridge. I was still too angry to speak to Ebenezer. Instead, I took a book from a shelf, and flicked through it as I ate. I was surprised to see an inscription at the front, written in my father's hand.

To my brother Ebenezer on his fifth birthday.

This confused me. I thought my father was Ebenezer's younger brother – how could he have written that well when he was so young?

Unless… Was my father older than Ebenezer? If so, then he should have inherited this estate. And that would mean that this house, and my uncle's money, belonged to me.

Ebenezer saw my frown as I read the inscription. "Give me that!" he shrieked. He sprang from his chair, and snatched the book from my hands. Then he threw that into the fire as well.

"You don't trust me, Davie."

"I certainly do not," I replied, stiffly. "Are you even the true lord of this estate?"

My uncle winced. Had I offended him, or scared him with the truth?

"What nonsense!" he said. "You must come with me to Queensferry. We can visit my lawyer, Mr. Rankeillor. He knew your father, and will put your mind at rest."

"Very well," I declared. "Lead the way."

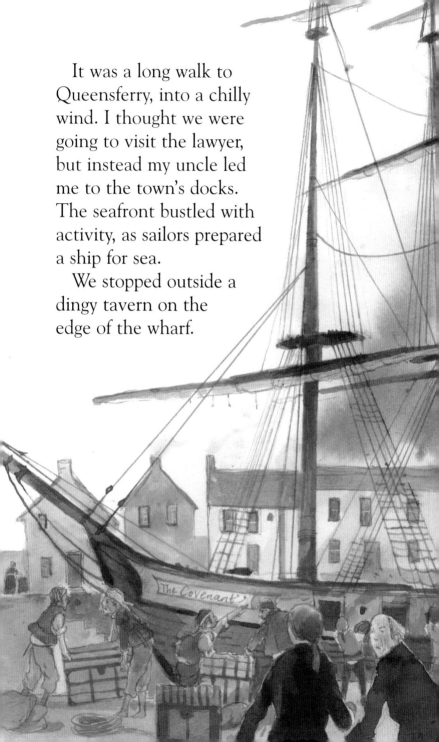

It was a long walk to Queensferry, into a chilly wind. I thought we were going to visit the lawyer, but instead my uncle led me to the town's docks. The seafront bustled with activity, as sailors prepared a ship for sea.

We stopped outside a dingy tavern on the edge of the wharf.

"I just have to take care of some business with the ship's captain," Ebenezer explained.

Inside, I watched my uncle meet with the captain – a big man with a brutal face, and tattoos on his arms. I wondered what sort of business Ebenezer could have with a man like that...

As I stood at the bar, the landlord eyed me suspiciously. "Did you come here with Ebenezer?" he said.

I told him that I did.

"Your face reminds me of his brother, Alexander," he replied.

He meant my father. "Did you know him?" I asked.

"Oh yes. Alexander was as good as Ebenezer is wicked. I heard that Ebenezer cheated him of his inheritance."

My suspicions were confirmed! And that meant the House of Shaws belonged to me. More than ever, I wanted to speak with this lawyer, Mr. Rankeillor. I set off from the tavern to find him.

As I marched along the dock, a voice called out. "Mr. Balfour!"

The captain strode from the inn. His face was red and flustered. "Do you have a moment to talk?" he asked. He leaned closer, and I smelled the beer on his breath. "It's about your uncle. I think he means you harm."

"What harm?" I asked.

"I will tell you in private, on my ship."

He led me on board, as his crew loaded the last crates for their voyage. The ship swayed, and the tall masts creaked and groaned.

"Now," I asked, "what harm does my uncle wish upon me?"

"This!" cried the captain.

Before I could react, he swung a plank at my head. I felt a sharp blow, like a thunderbolt, and collapsed to the deck.

My head swirled. My vision swam. Through blurry eyes, I saw the sailors cast off the ship's ropes. We were going to sea!

Just as I began to pass out, I saw my uncle watching from the dock. A cruel smile spread across his wrinkled face.

"No," I gasped. "No…"

And then I saw nothing.

Chapter 3

The outlaw Alan Breck

For three days, I drifted in and out of consciousness, locked in the belly of the ship. I overheard the crew on the deck, and learned that we were headed for America, where I would be sold as a slave.

There was nothing I could do – I was too weak to fight the crew alone. Instead, I curled up on the floor, sobbing pathetically. I should have been the lord of an estate, but now I faced a life of misery.

Once I had recovered, I was forced to work in the roundhouse – the cabin where the sailors ate. All day, I served the captain and his crew meals, and poured them drinks.

At night, I was kept awake by the violent sway of the ship on the waves. By the fifth day of my capture, the waves had grown even higher. I heard the crew shout and curse, as they struggled against a storm.

As I served the captain a drink, I sneaked a look at his sea chart. I was stunned to see how far the wind had forced us back – we were now only five miles from the coast of the Scottish Highlands.

Right at that moment, a mighty crash shook the wooden walls.

"We've hit a boat!" one of the crew yelled.

I rushed to the window, and was horrified to see a small dinghy sinking in the waves. There was no sign of its crew, except one man, who clung bravely to the front of our ship.

"Bring him aboard!" the captain ordered.

The man was rescued, and brought into the roundhouse.

He was a striking figure, with broad shoulders, and wide, twinkling eyes. He wore a flamboyant feathered hat, and a plush velvet coat that was decorated with silver buttons. The buttons clinked against a sword at his side.

The clothes looked French, but the man was Scottish. I guessed that he was a rebel – one of the Highlanders who fought against the British king and his army in Scotland.

"My apologies for your boat," the captain said, although he didn't sound sorry at all.

"Save them for its crew," the man replied, "who are at the bottom of the sea. In return, you can land me on the shore."

I saw the captain glance greedily at a purse in the man's pocket. I knew then that he planned to trick this man, just as he had tricked me.

"Wait here," the captain said. "I'll talk to my crew."

As soon as we were alone, I poured the man a drink. I leaned close, lowering my voice to a whisper. "They're going to kill you," I said.

The man sipped the drink coolly. "I suspected as much," he said. "And will you stand with me?"

At last, here was my opportunity to escape. Highland rebels were famous for their courage. Perhaps, with this man's help, I actually stood a chance against the crew. "I will," I said firmly.

The man grinned, and clapped me on the back. "Then I had better know your name."

"It is David Balfour, the true lord of the estate of Shaws."

I thought my title would impress him, but his grin grew wider.

"Well, David of the Shaws, my name is Alan Breck. But I don't have an estate to boast about."

I was embarrassed by his joke, but there was no time to worry about that now.

Alan Breck drew his sword. "How many sailors are there?" he asked.

"Fifteen," I told him. "They have swords, but we have all the guns."

Alan's eyes lit up as I showed him the chest where the crew stored their firearms.

"Ha!" he said. "Maybe we will survive the night after all."

He handed me a pistol, but my hand trembled with fear, and I could barely hold the weapon.

Just then I heard the thump of feet on the deck, as the captain and his crew charged at the roundhouse.

"Be brave, David of the Shaws," cried Alan. "Here they come!"

Chapter 4

Shipwreck

There was a mighty roar, and the first sailor burst through the door. I had never experienced a battle before, and I am ashamed to say that the man's savage cry made me freeze with fear.

But Alan didn't hesitate. He launched forward, whirling his sword. The steel blade glinted in the lamplight as he sunk the weapon deep into the man's chest.

More of the crew stormed inside, and I knew I had to act. I gathered my courage, gripped my pistol, and fired.

BOOM! Blood sprayed everywhere, and one of the sailors staggered back, clutching his arm.

Alan charged at the others, striking again with his sword. There was a clash of steel, and cries from the crew.

Quickly, I reloaded the gun. My next shot hit the wall, but it was enough to scare the attackers away. They turned and fled, dragging their dead crewmate with them.

My ears still rang from the gunshots. The weapon slipped from my hand, and clattered to the floor. I couldn't stop shaking.

Alan, though, looked delighted. He threw his arms around me in a tight hug. "You stood beside me in battle, Davie," he said. "I will never forget that. But it's not over yet. They'll soon be back."

I pulled on my coat, and we sat against the wall, waiting for the next attack. Alan spoke proudly about his life. He told me that he was from a clan named the Stewarts, who fought against King George and his army.

I felt embarrassed. I was from the Lowlands of Scotland, where most people supported the King.

Alan's face grew dark. "I tell you Davie," he said. "I curse any Highland clan that help the King. But the person I hate the most is the Red Fox – a Highlander who works for the King's army. He plans to force every Stewart from their home, and steal their land. You would know the Red Fox if you saw him, Davie, for he has long, flame-red hair."

He gripped the handle of his sword. "If I had the chance, I would murder that scoundrel right now."

The force in Alan's words startled me. He must have noticed, for his hand rose and gripped my shoulder.

"The Stewarts are loyal to each other, Davie," he said. "And now that we have fought together, they'll be loyal to you, too."

With his sword, he cut one of the buttons from his coat. He placed it in my hand, and I saw that it was decorated with an intricate, swirling pattern.

"Wherever you go in the Scottish Highlands," he said, "show that button, and my friends will help you."

Again, I felt my face redden with shame. I had hoped that a title after my name would make people respect me. All Alan needed to earn respect was a button.

I was about to thank him when the captain burst back into the roundhouse. His face had turned white with fear.

"The ship is in grave danger," he cried. "We need your help to control the sails, or we will be wrecked on the rocks."

Alan and I rushed outside, just as a huge wave washed over the deck. The fierce wind was already tearing the sails to shreds, and the ship lurched violently on the water.

In the moonlight, I saw that we were close to the coast. But, all around us, jagged rocks rose from the water, like the fangs of a giant sea monster.

"Hold on for your life, Davie!" Alan cried.

The ship slammed against the rocks. Wood shattered. Waves crashed. And we were all flung into the sea.

The dark water swallowed me, and then spat me back up. In a flash of lightning, I saw sailors drowning, and the wreck of the ship smashing against the rocks.

"Alan!" I screamed. But my cry was lost to a roar of thunder.

I grasped a plank, and clung on for my life. I kicked my legs as hard as I could until I felt sand under my feet. Shaking from cold and fear, I crawled onto the beach, and collapsed…

Chapter 5

The Red Fox

When I woke, the storm had passed and sunlight dazzled my eyes. Wreckage from the ship was strewn across the beach, but I could see no other survivors.

My lips were parched, and hunger gnawed at my belly. I felt so miserable and alone. But, far inland, a trail of smoke rose into the sky. Was it coming from a house?

As I staggered closer, I saw that it was more like a hut, in the middle of a wide, empty moor. A toothless old man sat outside, puffing on a pipe.

"Help!" I groaned. "My ship has been wrecked. Have you seen any other survivors?"

He plucked the pipe from his mouth, and blew a cloud of smoke. "Perhaps," he said.

I understood his reply. Alan Breck was a wanted outlaw. If this man was his friend, he would be wary of telling people that he'd seen him here.

I remembered Alan's button, and dug it from my pocket.

As soon as he saw it, the old man grinned. "The boy with the silver button!" he said.

"Where is Alan?" I asked eagerly.

"He has gone into the Highlands to hide. He told me that you might pass. Come inside and eat!"

I must have thanked that man a hundred times, as he stoked the fire to get me warm, and gave me hot porridge.

As I ate, I stared into the fire, and thought of my evil uncle. I was determined to get revenge against him, and claim my rightful inheritance. To do so, I would have to find the lawyer, Mr. Rankeillor, and hope that he believed my story. He lived in Queensferry, and that was a long walk from here, across wild Highland countryside. I wasn't sure that I was tough enough for that sort of journey, but I had to try.

The next day, I set off. Wrapped in a blanket, I tramped across fields of heather, and vast, desolate moors. The sky darkened, and freezing rain soaked my clothes. When the sun came out, biting flies swarmed around my face.

The walk was even harder than I had feared. But, wherever I showed Alan's button, I was greeted with warmth. His friends gave me food, drink, and beds by crackling fires.

As my journey went on, I began to feel more and more ashamed. I had always believed that Highlanders were wild people, who needed to be tamed. But, so far, I had only met kindness.

One morning, I came to some woods at the bottom of a craggy hill. A line of English soldiers marched along the path, brass buttons gleaming on their coats. They were led by a burly man, whose face was as red as his long, shaggy hair.

I realized with a shudder that this was the man that Alan had told me about – the Red Fox. The Red Fox and the soldiers were hunting for people who opposed King George, to throw them from their homes.

I stepped aside, hoping they would march past. But the Red Fox ordered the soldiers to stop. Then he stepped up to me, and jabbed me in the chest.

"You!" he said, with a sneer. "Are you loyal to the King, or to the rebels?"

I didn't know what to say. Although I was proud to be a friend of the rebel Alan Breck, if I said so now, I would be arrested. But, before I could answer…

BOOM!

A gunshot rang out from the woods. The Red Fox staggered back, and collapsed.

"He's been murdered!" cried a soldier.

A dark figure raced away between the trees. It was the killer! Several soldiers set off after him, but the others turned and aimed their rifles at me.

"This man is the killer's accomplice," one of them said.

One of the soldiers tried to grab me, but I dodged his grasp. I wanted to tell them I was innocent, but knew they wouldn't listen.

Instead, I fled between the trees. Bullets whizzed past my head, missing me by inches. Suddenly, it seemed as if there were soldiers everywhere. I was breathless with fear, barely able to think.

A hand grasped my arm. I cried out and turned to fight, and couldn't believe who I saw – Alan!

He pulled me behind a rock, just as several soldiers charged past, running deeper into the woods. Then Alan burst from our hiding place and raced up the hill. "Come on, Davie," he called.

I ran after him, scrambling over rocks. We stopped at the top of the hill, and lay down to catch our breath. Now that we were safe, my fear turned into anger. "Did you murder the Red Fox?" I demanded.

"It wasn't me," Alan said. "I came back to find you, Davie. I hated the Red Fox, but killing him would only bring more trouble upon my clan."

I could see in his eyes that he was telling the truth. "Then who did kill him?"

"I didn't see," Alan replied.

I knew he was lying to protect the killer. I didn't approve, but I respected his loyalty to his fellow outlaws.

"You are an outlaw too now, Davie," Alan told me. "Luckily the soldiers do not know your name. We must go south, to your part of Scotland, so you can reclaim your estate. Then you can help me find a ship to take me to France."

He gripped my arm firmly. "It won't be easy," he warned. "The English soldiers will hunt us like wild animals. Are you ready?"

I breathed in deeply, gathering what little courage I had left. "I am," I said.

Chapter 6

On the run

We hid during the day, in case the army spotted us. Then we moved at night, side-by-side through the misty moonlight. Sometimes we ran, sometimes we walked – up rocky hills, across fierce rivers, and along valleys strewn with granite boulders. Around us, wild mountains rose into the starry sky.

We slept for one day in a cave at the base of a mountain. For another day, we hid at the top of a hill, and watched soldiers in the valley below. They were searching for us.

The next night, we climbed one mountain after another, struggling against bitter winds. I felt dizzy with tiredness, but I kept going, determined not to let Alan down.

By sunrise, we reached a vast moor – a sea of purple heather. It was too light to keep going, but there was nowhere to hide.

"This is a dangerous place to stop," Alan muttered. "You sleep first, Davie, and I will keep watch."

I slept for three hours, curled up like a baby in the prickly heather. Alan woke me around noon, when the sun was directly overhead.

"Now you keep watch," he whispered.

He lay back, and seconds later I heard him snoring.

I sat beside him and tried to stay awake. But my eyes felt so heavy. The soft drone of the bees lulled me into a slumber… and I closed my eyes.

I jolted awake, and almost cried out in anger. I had broken Alan's trust and fallen asleep. And then I saw the soldiers!

A dozen men on horseback rode slowly in our direction, spread out across the moor.

I woke Alan, and felt so ashamed. He knew
I had fallen asleep, but he didn't mention it.

"Over there," he said, spotting a forest on
the other side of the moor. "If we can reach
those trees, we might be safe."

But, to do so, we would have to pass right
in front of the soldiers…

We didn't dare stand up. Instead, we slid on our stomachs like snakes. Jagged stones cut our bellies, and the spiky heather scratched our faces.

We got closer to the woods, but the soldiers got closer to us, too.

Now one of them was only twenty yards away…

Now he was ten yards from us…

My heart pounded so hard I was sure it would give us away. But the horse kept riding – the soldier didn't see us.

"Now!" Alan whispered.

We rose and sprinted into the woods. We ran and ran, stumbling like old men. We didn't stop until the sun disappeared from the sky, and darkness settled again over the Highlands.

Finally, we flopped into the long grass.

"We're safe now," Alan wheezed.

I lay beside him, my legs aching with exhaustion. We were still alive, but only just. And I feared there were more dangers ahead.

Chapter 7

Back home

We rested for a day, to recover our strength. Then we hiked again through the night. The weather grew even colder, but I felt stronger with each step. We had left the Highlands, and entered the Scottish Lowlands. I was close to home.

"We're not safe yet, Davie," Alan warned. "We need to find the lawyer, Mr. Rankeillor, and hope that he believes your story."

By morning, we had reached Queensferry. We rested on the roadside, watching smoke rise in lazy lines from the chimneys of the stone houses.

We were both wanted outlaws, and risked being caught if we entered a town. But I still felt ashamed for letting Alan down before, and knew this was my chance to make it up to him.

"I will go alone," I said. "You stay here, where it is safe."

Alan knew not to argue. He grasped my shoulder, and smiled warmly. "I love you like a brother, Davie. Good luck!"

My heart thumped as I entered Queensferry. It was an elegant market town, so I stood out in my dirty clothes. But, finally, I found the house I was looking for.

I knocked on the door, and was greeted by a man in a powdered wig and spectacles. It was Mr. Rankeillor.

"Can I help?" he asked.

At first, I was too scared to speak. If I told this lawyer my story, he might have me arrested. But I remembered Alan's courage in the Highlands, and stood up straight.

"My name is David Balfour," I declared. "I am the true lord of the House of Shaws."

The lawyer's eyes widened. "You had better come in," he said.

He led me into a dusty room, with books on shelves around the walls. "Now, tell me your story," he said, as he sat behind a desk.

So, I told him everything that had happened – the shipwreck, the murder of the Red Fox, my journey through the Highlands, and how my uncle Ebenezer had cheated me of my inheritance.

After I had finished, Mr. Rankeillor sat in silence for a minute, with his eyes closed. It felt like an eternity…

Then he sprang from his seat, and smiled. "You have been on an epic journey, David," he said. "Why, you've trekked across half of Scotland!"

"You… You believe me?" I asked, fearing this was a trick.

"Of course I do! I know your uncle, and I have no doubt that he is capable of such wickedness. I used to work for Ebenezer, until I discovered what a scoundrel he was."

I was so relieved to hear this that I had to sit down. "So what should I do?"

Mr. Rankeillor thought about it for a moment, and then his grin grew wider.

"You must plan a trick of your own on Ebenezer. You need to make him admit his crime. But, for that, you will need help from someone very daring…"

Now I smiled too, for the first time in weeks. "I know just the person," I said.

Chapter 8

Revenge

Later that night, Alan Breck strolled casually to the front door of my uncle's crumbling mansion, and banged on the door.

Close by, I hid with Mr. Rankeillor in some bushes. Alan glanced over at us, and winked. I couldn't help grinning in reply – our plan was underway.

The door creaked open. I felt a flush of anger when I saw Uncle Ebenezer again, pointing his gun at Alan. But Mr. Rankeillor gripped my arm, urging me to stay hidden. We had to let Alan talk…

"Who are you?" my uncle demanded.

Alan smiled calmly. "I have come about David," he said.

Ebenezer's gun trembled, and his eyes twitched. "D…David?" he stuttered.

"I am from the Isle of Mull," Alan said, repeating the story we had created. "There was a shipwreck there, and a survivor washed up on the beach. My clan have locked him in our castle's dungeon, and I am here to demand a ransom for his release."

Alan sounded so convincing that I almost believed his story myself.

"Keep him in your castle," Ebenezer said, with a cruel grin.

"We can't do that," Alan replied. "If you won't pay, then we will have to kill him. Is that what you want?"

The smile spread wider across my uncle's face, and I knew he was thinking of saying yes. But he shook his head. "How much would I have to pay you to keep him locked up?" he asked.

"Well," Alan said, "how much did you pay for David to be kidnapped? That is what you did, isn't it?"

Ebenezer shrugged. "I did, and I'm not sorry. I gave the captain twenty pounds. Is that enough for you?"

As soon as my uncle said this, Mr. Rankeillor leaped from our hiding place. "That is quite enough for *me*, Mr. Balfour!" he shouted.

Now I stepped into the moonlight too. "Good evening," I said.

Ebenezer's face turned as pale as the moon.

My uncle knew he'd been tricked into confessing his crime. He stood in the doorway, like a man turned to stone.

We led him into the kitchen, and sat him at the table.

Mr. Rankeillor had prepared a document that gave the house, and all of Ebenezer's money, to me. My uncle knew that he had to sign it, or else he would face prison. Once he had, we took him upstairs, and locked him in his bedroom.

Alan and Mr. Rankeillor poured drinks, and we celebrated our victory. I decided to let Ebenezer stay here, although now I was the lord of this house. But I didn't really care about having a title any more. I knew, from my time with Alan, that it was a man's actions that proved his worth.

The next day, I walked with Alan to Edinburgh. My adventure was over, but he still had a long journey ahead. I gave him some money to pay for his voyage to France, and prayed he would make it there safely.

We walked slowly, and in silence. As the sun set, we stopped on top of a hill and looked out across Edinburgh and the sea. Alan took my hand.

"Goodbye," he said, "David of the Shaws."

I cleared my throat, hoping Alan didn't hear the emotion in my voice. "Goodbye, Alan," I replied.

As I watched him walk away, I thought of all the adventures we had been through together. I would miss my friend, the outlaw Alan Breck.

I felt so sad right then that I wanted to cry. But I knew Alan wouldn't approve. I was a man now, and I had to act like one. So I stood up straight, fastened my coat, and set off back to my new home.

Robert Louis Stevenson
1850-1894

Robert Louis Stevenson was born in Scotland in 1850. From a young age he suffered fevers brought on by the cold Scottish weather, so he spent much of his life overseas. His travels inspired him to write plays, poems and popular adventure stories such as *Kidnapped*, and *Treasure Island*. These made him one of the most famous writers of the 19th century. He died, aged 44, on a small island in the Pacific Ocean.

Designed by Caroline Spatz
Series editor: Lesley Sims
Series designer: Russell Punter

First published in 2012 by Usborne Publishing Ltd., Usborne House, 83-85 Saffron Hill, London EC1N 8RT, England. www.usborne.com
Copyright © 2012 Usborne Publishing Ltd.